JACKIE WINQUACKEY

And Her 43 CATS

Go To

HOLLYWOOD

by Jessie Lynch Frees

Illustrated by Jaroslav "Jerry" Gebr
Art Director Verne Nobles Sr.

tizbit ®
Quality Books for Children

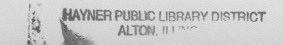

First Edition 2005

Text Copyright © 2005 by Jessie Lynch Frees
Illustration Copyright © 2005
All rights reserved.

Published in the United States by
Tizbit Books, LLC.
304 Route 22 West
Springfield, NJ 07081

www.tizbitbooks.com

Printed in Singapore

Library of Congress Control Number: 2004111501

ISBN 0-9760553-0-9
10 9 8 7 6 5 4 3 2 1

To my grandchildren:
Jacqueline, Greg, Elizabeth, Jonathan,
Stephen, Matthew, Michael and Mark.

Ms. Jackie Winquackey
had forty-three cats.
They often would gather
to have cozy chats.

Cats sat on her dresser,
her bed and her chair,
in her closet and bathtub,
cats slept everywhere.

Jackie Winquackey
was sitting one day,
just watching her cats
rehearse for a play.

The cats were great actors,
not one sang off-key.
They often were featured
on cable TV.

A talent scout saw them
and called up to say,
"We want you for movies,
come quick to L.A.!"

"My cats have such talent,"
Ms. Jackie would boast,
"They should be in movies,
we'll fly to the coast."

They promptly agreed
to become movie stars.
"We'll buy lots of cat toys
and drive fancy cars."

The cats were excited
and thought it was groovy,
to be featured as stars
in a HOLLYWOOD MOVIE!

They arrived at the airport,
each nose in the air.
People were staring,
the cats didn't care.

When buying the tickets
folks whispered, "She's bats...
reserving THOSE seats
for the forty-three cats!"

Each cat had a window,
she paid extra fare,
so the cats could look out
when they flew through the air.

A fidgety passenger
started to fret,
when she saw that each cat
had a seat on the jet.

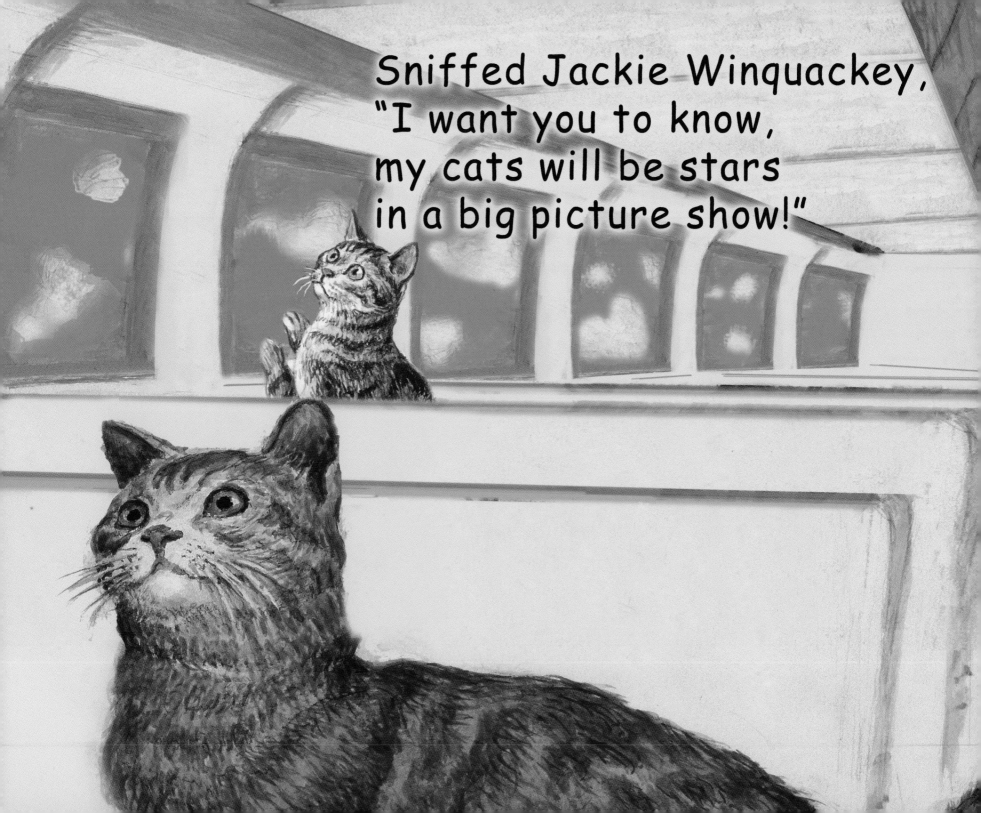

With the seatbelt sign off,
the cats left their seats,
they ran down the aisles
just looking for treats.

A stewardess chased them
all over the plane,
she hissed to a steward,
"These cats are a pain!"

They slipped into First Class,
"We'd rather sit here!
These seats are more comfy
than those in the rear."

One jumped on a tray,
which made a man scream.
The cat spilled his coffee
and lapped up the cream.

When the plane finally landed the pilots and crew breathed a sigh of relief and bid them adieu.

They starred in a film,
which took six months to make.
The director was pleased
as he okayed each take.

Scene 1
Take 2
Roll 3

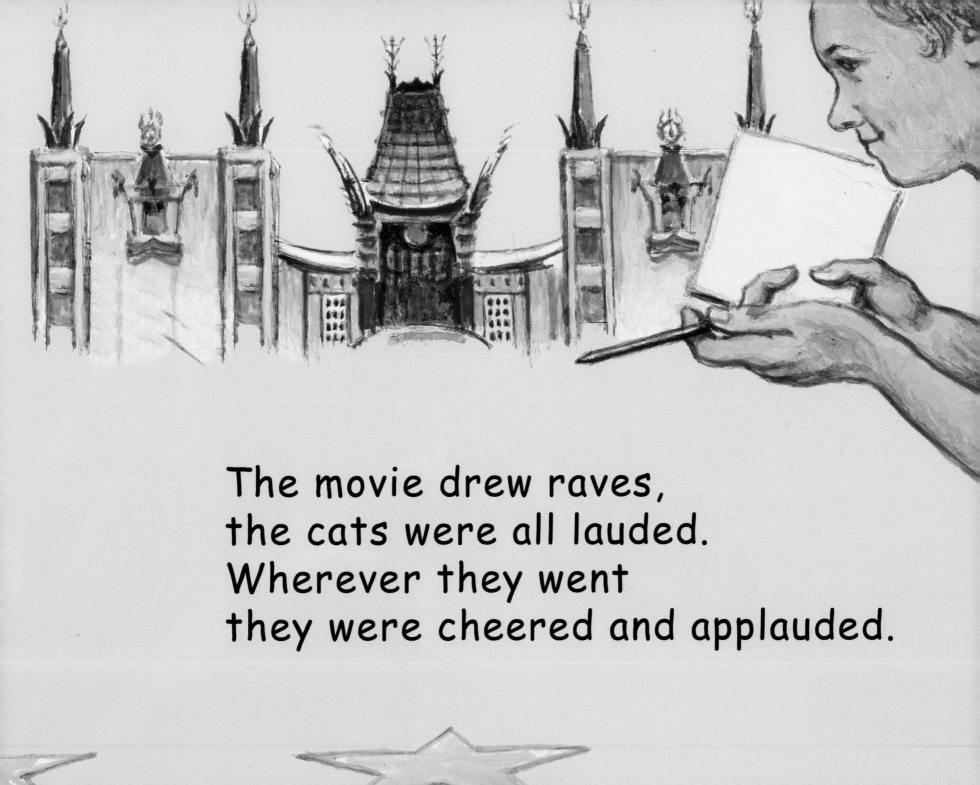

The movie drew raves,
the cats were all lauded.
Wherever they went
they were cheered and applauded.

And when they flew back
from their glamorous trip,
the cats had the last laugh,
they thought it a rip.

They sat in their seats,
the cats were not straying.
We'll give you three guesses
what movie was playing...

Award-winning veteran radio talk show host, Jessie Frees, has interviewed thousands of notable guests in her 35-year broadcast career. She currently hosts two live call-in talk shows, "Your New Jersey Connection" and "Ask The Expert." A mother of three, and grandmother of eight, she enjoys traveling, reading and spending time at her summer home on the Jersey Shore.

Jaroslav "Jerry" Gebr, received his formal training in Europe. His paintings and scenic art have been featured in a broad range of classic motion pictures such as *The Sound of Music*, *My Fair Lady*, *Batman*, *Star Trek* and *The Princess Diaries*. Jerry has worked with many of the industry's top directors, including John Badham, Clint Eastwood and Steven Spielberg. He is perhaps best known for his distinctive title work for *The Sting*, starring Paul Newman and Robert Redford.

Verne Nobles, a 40 year veteran of the entertainment industry is an award winning writer, producer, director, designer and artist. A grandfather of 15, he has dedicated his life to family entertainment.